Jackson Jones and the Puddle of Thorns

YEARLING BOOKS are designed especially to entertain and enlighten young people. Patricia Reilly Giff, consultant to this series, received her bachelor's degree from Marymount College and a master's degree in history from St. John's University. She holds a Professional Diploma in Reading and a Doctorate of Humane Letters from Hofstra University. She was a teacher and reading consultant for many years, and is the author of numerous books for young readers.

For a complete listing of all Yearling titles, write to
Dell Readers Service,
P.O. Box 1045,
South Holland, IL 60473.

Jackson Jones and the Puddle of Thorns

Mary Quattlebaum

ILLUSTRATED BY
Melodye Rosales

A Yearling Book

Published by
Bantam Doubleday Dell Books for Young Readers
a division of
Bantam Doubleday Dell Publishing Group, Inc.
1540 Broadway
New York, New York 10036

ISBN: 0-440-41066-5

Reprinted by arrangement with Delacorte Press
Printed in the United States of America

May 1995

10   9   8   7   6   5   4   3   2

To Christopher,
my partner in the garden

Jackson Jones and the Puddle of Thorns

1

Every success story has a beginning. But I wonder if those great folks *knew* when they had taken the first step down that road. Like there was a sign: GREATNESS—NEXT RIGHT.

For example, George Washington. He chopped down that cherry tree and owned right up to it. Did he say to himself: "Here's the beginning of my success story, so I better not blow it by lying"? Or did he try to fix that tree? And squeak out real fast to his daddy: "I-chopped-down-the-tree-with-my-little-hatchet-but-it-was-looking-*bad*"?

To puzzle out the answer I've read my share of books on good-doing folks. And believe me, there are lots. Athletes, presidents, artists. Black, white, yellow. All inspiring.

And I figure, the writers left out a lot.

Such as when the GREAT ONES were bad in school. And wasted money on video games. And smacked kid sisters.

For once, I would like to read a story about a real guy who was not always so GREAT.

So I decided to write about myself. Not that I'm GREAT (yet, anyway). But I was pretty successful last summer.

And let me tell you, getting there was not so great.

The story begins on my tenth birthday.

2

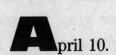

April 10.

Jackson-Jones-Born-into-This-World Day. I was moving from nine to almost grown. Double digits. The Big 1-0. The Man (that's me) is TEN.

My best friend, Reuben, was impressed. He's nine and counting. One hundred and thirty-two days till he's ten.

"What ya going to get for your birthday?" he asked. He sketched the star on Captain Nemo's helmet. I was sprawled on his bed.

I shrugged, acting cool. Like saying, "Oh, is it my *birth*day?" Acting like I didn't know Mama was rattling my favorite Red Velvet cake into the oven. HOPEFULLY wrapping a new basketball.

That's what I wanted, a basketball.

The one I had was so old, it didn't bounce anymore. Just sort of *thuck*ed.

Thuck. Thuck. Thuck. *Not* the way to dribble.

"What you need is a basketball," said Reuben, honing in on my thoughts, "to replace that orange Frisbee you call a ball." He pencil-shaded Nemo's star a precise gray. "Remind me to ask for paints for my birthday," he added, "so I can give Nemo some color."

Captain Nemo Comics by Jackson Jones and Reuben Casey is our life's work. I write. He draws. We're the perfect team. We've taken Captain Nemo to Planet Huzarconi, which is ringed with deadly gases. He's fought the six-headed Cerebral and the no-armed Flawt. And we've got about 293 Nemo adventures left to do. I figure Reuben and I will be the perfect team until we're old, old men.

Reuben carefully drew a bubble from Captain Nemo's mouth.

I dug into my pocket, unfolded a piece of

paper, and read: "Begone, evil wizard, lest I smite you."

Reuben printed *Begone* in the bubble. Stopped.

"Do people say 'Begone'?"

"Of course not," I said. " 'Begone' is hero talk."

Reuben said "Begone" to himself three times.

Did I say we were the perfect team? Excuse me, I meant to say *slightly less than* perfect. What holds us back from one hundred percent perfection is this: Reuben is soooo careful. And slow.

Mama says Reuben is the careful tortoise and I am the impatient hare in that story where the turtle wins the race and the rabbit looks like a fool.

That story makes no sense. I can beat Reuben at any race. But sometimes I slow down so he almost wins. When I tell this to Mama, she just says, "Maybe that rabbit's so bent on winning, he can't see there's no race." I think Mama's explanation twists the story—but still makes no sense.

Reuben was still muttering "Begone" when the phone rang.

His grandma, Miz Lady, answered it.

"I'm not sure Jackson wants a tenth birthday," she said, loud so I'd hear. "He's acting mighty cool."

I grinned. Miz Lady was acting cool herself. She knew inside I was balloons and basketballs.

"Your mama says your birthday is ready, Mister Cool." She flapped her hands at me and Reuben. "I'll be along as soon as I find your present." She peered into a closet. "Now, where did I *put* it?"

"It's under your bed," Reuben whispered loudly.

"What?"

"UNDER YOUR BED." Reuben let out the loudest whisper I'd ever heard. Miz Lady's hearing is not too good. That's why she hollers so much. She thinks other folks' ears are just as bad.

I slouched out the door, moving slooooww. Letting some of Reuben's turtle rub off on me. I wanted this birthday to last a looong time.

"Ten," said Reuben, naturally walking slow. "All right."

Walking slooowwly, I had lots of time to think. My first thought: Apartments are the perfect way to live. Reuben and Miz Lady are down the hall in Apartment 316. I knew that in 506 Juana Rivera was sneaking away from her kid sister, Gaby, and her tagalong brother, Ro. And Abraham was slinking out of 219 as his mother hollered, "Remember, sweetie, just a teensy piece of cake." Even our mailman lived in Apartment 102 and sometimes delivered the mail right into my hand.

Everyone was coming to Apartment 302. Coming for my tenth birthday.

Except Mailbags Mosely, on account of being in college at night. But this morning he had clapped a Chicago Bulls starters cap on my head and grinned a happy birthday. Yeah. Now all I needed was the basketball.

I was walking so slowly, I was almost stopped.

Cake smell, smooth and chocolate, tried to hurry my steps.

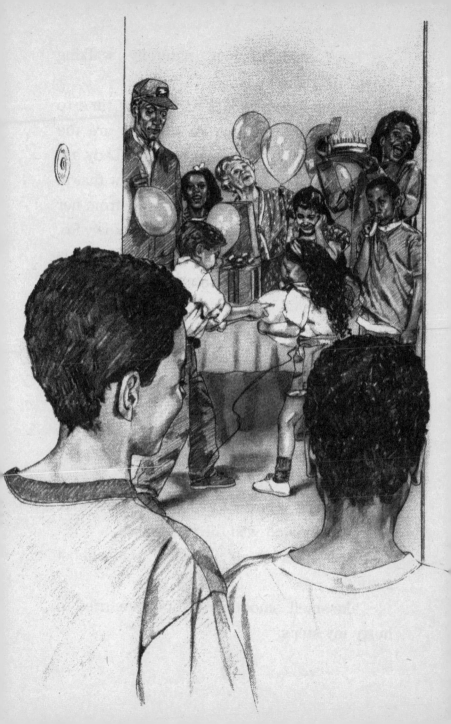

Reuben and I moved like two snails. Like two snails going backward.

Till I couldn't stand such slowness any longer. I jumped for Apartment 302, flung open the door.

Birthday!

Balloons. A cake stuck with candles till it looked like a porcupine. I shifted my eyes casually over the present pile. No basketball shape wrapped in blue paper.

But there was an envelope with my name in Mama's writing.

Money! Cartoon dollar signs flipped in my head. Mama was giving me money to buy just what I wanted.

After ten years of "Jackson, you know we don't have the money for that."

After ten years of "We don't have a coupon for that kind of cereal. Put it back."

After ten years of "You'd think dollars were toilet paper, they go that fast."

Mama was giving me money for my birthday. I felt truly grown up.

Juana waved from the kitchen. Abraham

eyeballed the cake. Miz Lady flapped her present like a fan.

Mama arranged all her plants around the cake, like invited guests. She fussed with their leaves.

Mama says talking to plants makes them grow. They can *sense* when you're kind, she says. It sounds cuckoo, I know. But her African violets are fuzzier, her philodendron is wider, and her ivy clambers about like a jungle. I've about given up being embarrassed.

See, Mama grew up in the country and never got over it. "Sheer heaven," she always sighs. "Miles of green grass, roses, cows, my own horse. The city is no place for a boy."

Personally, I think the country sounds like the *opposite* of heaven. Who wants to tug some old cow's bag when he could shoot hoops? But Mama's stuck on country-land. She even named me Jackson, after her old horse.

Still, Jackson is a good name, horse or no horse. What if she'd called me Bossy?

Every mother has her weirdness, I figure. Abraham's mother watches over him like a worried bird. The only time he can eat cake or unwashed carrots is when he visits Reuben or me. I'll take Mama's plant-yakking any day.

Abraham lit the candles. Everyone sang, "Happy birthday, dee-aa-rrr Jackson," and I made a wish.

You guessed it. I wished for a basketball. But it was an I-got-this-wish-in-the-bag kind of wish, instead of an eyes-squeezed-want-it-with-all-my-heart wish. I *knew* I was getting that b-ball.

"I keep waiting for *them* to appear," said Juana.

She gobbled her cake as if *they* might suddenly appear and snatch it away. "Yesterday I took one of those stress tests at People's Drug. You press a dot and the color changes. Blue means relaxed; red means totally whacked out. Mine was *crimson*. Those kids made me a basket case."

"Gaby and Ro might calm down in a few years," said Mama.

"Where's your basketball?" Reuben whispered to me.

11

I ignored him. I ate my cake very slooowwly.

"Mister Cool," hollered Miz Lady, "don't you think it's time you opened those presents?"

I untied ribbon and peeled tape so slooowwly, the wrapping paper didn't rip at all. That paper could wrap up next year's presents.

I got socks from Abraham ("Mom picked them out," he said. "Sorry."); a glow-in-the-dark armband from Juana; and a Georgetown Hoyas T-shirt from Reuben and Miz Lady.

I carefully folded the wrapping paper.

"There's one more," said Mama.

I gave her my best Is-it-my-*birth*day? look. Reuben rolled his eyes.

Mama held the envelope like a little white bird. Stuffed with money, I couldn't help thinking.

"Ten years ago," said Mama, stroking the bird-money, "God gave *me* a present: my son, Jackson. Each year I grow prouder of him."

I was cool, just taking it in. Thinking about slam-dunking my new b-ball.

"I always wanted Jackson to have the kind of childhood I had," Mama continued.

Wait a minute. Mama had no basketball in that country childhood. Her best friend lived seven miles away.

Mama handed me the envelope. Her eyes were all misty-happy.

"Jackson, I hope you enjoy this gift as much as I enjoyed mine as a girl."

Forget slooowwly. I snatched the envelope. Clawed the flap.

I drew out the card. Opened it.

I couldn't believe what I saw.

3

Noise pushed at me.

"Do you like it?" from Mama.

"Ain't Mr. Cool excited now?" from Miz Lady.

"What is it?" from Juana.

"Plot five one," I answered all of them.

"A plot in the Rooter's Community Garden on Evert Street." Mama beamed.

I knew Rooter's. I must have passed it a billion times and never felt the urge to open the chain-link gate and join all those sweating, digging, grunting garden people. Mailbags Mosely even had a plot and gave us tomatoes each year. "Sweeter than store-bought"—he'd smack his lips. But I couldn't taste a difference. And who cared?

Now I was a Rooter.

"There's ten dollars in the card for seeds, manure, and tools," said Mama. "I'm as excited as if this was *my* garden."

I wished it was.

"I don't know anything about gardens" was all I said.

"Oh, gardening is easy," said Mama. "All you do is plant the seeds and—"

"Talk to 'em."

"See, you're a pro already." Mama looked at me anxiously. "Do you like your present?"

"Sure." I figured the present could be worse. I might have gotten a cow or a "vacation" in the country with rope swings, fishing poles, and other country-doing things.

But my tenth birthday had flattened like a basketball hit by a Mack truck. POP!-fssssss.

Mama answered a knock at the door.

Maybe some razzle-dazzle player would dribble through. He'd juke and leap and send a birthday b-ball straight into my hands. "Surprise!" everyone would yell.

But instead, a dervish whirled right for the cake, separated into two parts, and clung to Juana. I groaned. Gaby and Ro Rivera.

Juana is about the smartest kid I know. She can speak English *and* Spanish, at the same time even, and not get them mixed up. Her parents came from Colombia and still speak Spanish. Juana's tried to teach me a few words.

She can even understand Gaby and Ro, who usually chatter at the same time. And because they're little—Gaby's six years old and Ro's four—they sometimes use the wrong words. To figure out their speech Juana must be brilliant.

Now the kids wanted cake.

"Just a little piece," said Juana.

The devouring duo hurled themselves at the paper plates, gobbled the cake, grabbed Juana, and dragged her out the door. Juana didn't even struggle. She looked like a prisoner resigned to her fate.

"What are you going to plant in your garden, Jackson?" Miz Lady asked.

"Oh, flowers," sighed Mama, gliding the

cake into the kitchen. "Marigolds, zinnias, nas-turtiums."

I was wrong. My birthday could get worse. Who ever heard of a basketball star with a summer bouquet?

Reuben shot me a look that said, What you gonna do now?

Mama came back with packets of cake for Miz Lady, Reuben, and Abraham. Abraham would have to eat his quickly—before his mother snatched it.

"Happy Birthday, Mister Cool," Miz Lady hollered as she left.

"Nas-tur-tiums." Reuben shook his head.

Then I got a brilliant idea. Not just brilliant—spectacular. How to have a garden and a basketball too. Or, rather, how to have a bas-ketball because of a garden. My deflated day started pumping back up again.

"A garden." Mama smiled to her pot of be-gonias.

A garden. Already, I could picture myself dribbling down a wide-open court. Fast. Smooth. And not a flower in sight.

. . .

"Nas-tur-tiums," Reuben repeated the next day. "They even sound nasty."

He was back at his desk, drawing. I was sprawled on his bed. Our favorite working position.

"A garden. What kind of present is *that* for a tenth birthday?" Reuben shook his head.

Then a look of horror crossed his face.

"Do you think Miz Lady would give me a garden—"

"Relax," I said. "Your birthday's in August. Gardens are almost over by then."

"Re*lief*," said Reuben. He paused, drew a finicky line, erased it. "You gonna tell your mama you don't want it?"

Very coolly I said, "Maybe I do want it."

"What!" Reuben shot up so fast, he forgot he was slow. "You *want* nas-turtiums and marigolds and that other thing?"

"Zinnias."

"You *want* zinnias?" he howled. "Man, turning ten turned your brain. What you gonna do with flowers?"

"Sell them."

"Sell them," Reuben said slowly. I could

almost see his mind puzzling the idea of planting flowers, selling flowers, buying . . .

"What you gonna buy?"

"Basketball," I said. "Wilson's best at twenty-four ninety-five. Shoot, I'll buy two basketballs. A hundred basketballs. One rose at Mabel's Fantastic Florals costs five dollars. We sell twelve roses—that's sixty bucks."

"You know nothing about growing flowers."

"It's easy. All you gotta do is plant some seeds and, um, talk to them."

"Man, you gonna talk to *seeds*?"

Outside I was very cool. Inside I was squirming. "Maybe we can take turns."

"Oh, now you want *me* to chat up some plants." Reuben stuck his pencil before his nose and chirped: "Good day, Mr. Zinnia! Are we ready to grow, grow, grow?" He crossed his eyes and resumed drawing the twelve zippers on Captain Nemo's uniform.

I leaned back on the bed, so cool I'm almost an ice cube. I started talking, like I was talking to myself.

"Bet I can grow fifty—no, a hundred roses.

And how much is five dollars times one hundred?"

Reuben was still drawing, very carefully.

"That's five hundred dollars for roses," I continued. "And I'll charge one dollar for each zinnia and whatever."

Reuben made tiny pencil strokes like he's fashioning the most careful zipper known to man.

I let my voice get so quiet, it's almost silence. "I wonder if Abraham and Juana would like to earn some extra money?"

"Jack-son," exploded Reuben, "I never said I wouldn't help you plant your flowers. But I *refuse* to talk to 'em."

"Maybe Juana will do the talking. Girls are supposed to like flowers."

"When do we start?"

"Tomorrow. We'll buy some seeds, stick them in the ground. Presto!—flowers."

Reuben thought. "I don't think a garden works like that. We gotta make a plan. You know, to decide what goes where."

Reuben drew a square precisely in the middle of the page. With a ruler he drew six dotted rows. All this took exactly eight minutes and forty-two seconds. (I checked my watch.)

Then he erased his first line and redid the dots. Another one minute and nine seconds.

"Reuben, man, it'll be July before you finish that plan. We gotta decide how much money to invest in seeds."

Reuben looked with satisfaction at his square and dots. "I got two dollars and fifty-seven cents."

"And I've got my ten-dollar birthday money, plus one dollar and eleven cents." I figured rapidly. "All in all that's thirteen dollars and sixty-eight cents."

"You two," Miz Lady bellowed from her chair by the TV. "I don't hear homework being done. You drawing that Nemo character?"

"No, we're not drawing *Captain* Nemo," said Reuben. "We're planning our garden."

"Oh, that's *nice*," Miz Lady hollered.

"And we're doing some math," I shouted back.

"Even better. Now, don't bother me. This

lady on the TV is about to win a refrigerator and some Stove Top stuffing."

I figured I'd never understand Miz Lady. Drawing Captain Nemo was a waste of time, but drawing a garden was *nice*.

"Be sure and plant some roses," yelled Miz Lady over the TV's hollering. "I do love a beautiful rose."

Reuben and I high-fived.

4

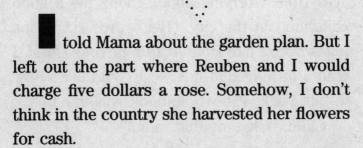

I told Mama about the garden plan. But I left out the part where Reuben and I would charge five dollars a rose. Somehow, I don't think in the country she harvested her flowers for cash.

Mama smiled. "Jackson, this is wonderful. I had a hard time deciding whether to give you a basketball or a garden. I wish I had enough money to give you both. But I thought you'd get so much more enjoyment out of a garden."

Yeah, right.

"You do like the garden, don't you?" Mama asked.

Mama is always anxious about raising me

right. See, my father ran off when I was a baby and she worries about me having no male role model. (She got that from TV.) I tell her I have Mailbags Mosely to role-model me. And she tells me not to bother him 'cause he's-working-full-time-and-going-to-college-and-don't-have-time-to-hardly-breathe-poor-man. I just shrug when she says that.

Mama has a little frown line between her eyes from worrying about giving me a good childhood in the city. (Her words.) And she reads books like *How to Talk to Your Child*. I read a little of that one, so I could learn how to talk back. The whole book was like this:

Child: "Give me that radio."

Parent: "You are behaving inappropriately."

Child (screaming): "I want that radio."

Parent: "You are behaving inappropriately."

Boring. Also stupid. I couldn't talk that mean to my mama. She'd probably start crying. And Miz Lady would clobber me.

So when she looked at me with that little

worry frown, I said, "Mama, the garden was a *good* present."

The worry frown disappeared. She smiled. "I can hardly wait to see the first seedlings. Why, the flowers should be blooming by June."

Then I got another brilliant idea. More than brilliant—spectacular.

Mama's birthday was in June.

I would give her the garden for her birthday.

Or, rather, her birthday present would be her first glimpse of all those marigolds, zinnias, and roses. Then I would chop them off and sell them for a profit.

I figured I must be a genius. *Plus* an excellent businessman. *Plus* a wonderful son.

I grinned. I could hardly wait for planting time.

I surveyed the rows of hoses, gloves, planters, hoes, shovels, and minishovels in Juniper's Hardware. And the prices: $6.95, $4.95, $.89, $8.57.

With his artist's eye Reuben was checking out the seven neat rows of seed packets.

Gaby and Ro were running around a tin garden shed, with Juana chasing them.

Immediately, a salesman materialized. One minute—nothing. Next minute—Poof!—some frosty-face Joe pops up like a magic trick.

"Stop that," he hissed.

That just made Gaby and Ro run faster.

Salesclerks come in two varieties: the kind that get cute with kids and the kind that treat kids like JDs. Frosty Joe was the second type. "Juvenile delinquent" flashed in his eyes when he looked at me.

I eyed all those hoses, hoes, et cetera, et cetera, again. Mr. Frosty Joe tapped his shiny shoe. Then I unfolded my list—as slooowwly as Reuben on his slowest day.

Gaby and Ro suddenly shot past and swarmed up the shelves. They dug their sneakers into the coiled hoses as if they were scaling a cliff.

Juana hurled some Spanish up at them. They spat words back. I'd catch a *"diablo"* and an *"agua"* once in a while but pretty much lost the conversation. I vowed to learn more Spanish.

I smiled my friendliest smile at Frosty Joe. "I'd like to see your rose seeds, please."

"Roses grow on bushes, young man." Frosty Joe squinted past me to Reuben. He figured I was trying to distract him while Reuben stuffed the seeds into his pocket. I felt mad, but I kept cool.

"Show me the bushes, then."

Frosty squeezed up his eyes like he had a headache and led me to a shelf crammed with bags of thorns.

Now I was suspicious. "Where's the flowers?"

"You want instant roses"—he actually sniffed—"go to a florist."

Reuben waved a seed packet at me and mouthed, "Zinnias."

Frosty Joe squinted at Reuben and then at me, like he was trying to crack a secret code.

He opened his mouth.

At that moment Gaby and Ro launched themselves from the fourth shelf. BANG! They hit that tin shed like Dorothy's tornado in *The*

Wizard of Oz. The shed folded in perfectly, like a box.

Salesclerks swarmed up the aisles. Frosty's face froze into the color of a grape Popsicle.

But Gaby and Ro had strategy.

They held tightly to Juana's hands. Tears slipped down their cheeks. Ro sucked his thumb artistically.

The salesclerks turned as sweet as pudding.

"Poor dears," cooed a saleswoman. Ro squeezed out a few more tears.

"Should we sue?" Gaby whispered to Juana.

The saleswoman enfolded each kid into a hug.

Juana escaped.

"Are Gaby and Ro okay?" Reuben asked.

"They're indestructible," said Juana. "They were trying to be raindrops, you know, falling on a window. Like in that kid's song."

"They're more like bombs dropping from the sky."

I hefted a minishovel.

"That's a spade," hissed Frosty.

Brrrr. It's April and the atmosphere in Juniper's Hardware is definitely *not* spring. I grabbed a book called *Easy Gardening* and a few seed packets and asked Reuben to help me lift a bag of fertilizer.

Reuben read the fine print on the bag. "Hey, man," he blurted, "this fertilizer is nothing but—"

"I know."

"You're going to pay four dollars for doo-doo?"

"It's an investment," I said. "The flowers grow bigger."

"What's that thorn tree?"

"Rosebush."

Reuben flicked the $4.95 price tag. "I hope you know what you're doing."

I gritted my teeth. Sometimes Reuben's slooowww carefulness got on my nerves. But it's best not to argue with a business partner, so I kept my mouth shut.

Gaby and Ro scampered up with suckers and pawed Juana.

"Let's get out of here before they wreck something else," Juana whispered to me.

I waved good-bye to Frosty Joe.

He didn't wave back.

Outside the store Gaby and Ro screamed to the end of the sidewalk, teetered on the curb, screamed back, circled us three times. Screamed.

"Don't they ever run into traffic?" Reuben asked, dragging the fertilizer.

"They have the survival instincts of sewer rats," Juana replied.

I held the rosebush straight out in front. It looked like a hostile being from Captain Nemo's planet.

One more block to the garden.

Before you knew it, those flowers would be shooting up.

And I'd be shooting hoops.

Yeah.

"Hey, Jones." The familiar voice shook me out of my daydream.

"Hey, Joooonesy." The voice squeaked into high pitch. "Has Joooonesy got hisself a cutesy flower?"

Gaby and Ro stopped screaming and stuck their thumbs in their mouths.

Reuben and Juana halted.

"Oh, Joooonesy," the voice continued. "I'm calling youuuu."

I hated that voice.

5

That voice belonged to Blood Green.

His real name was Howard, but about a year ago he changed it to "Blood" and beat up anyone (except his mother) who called him Howard. Since he's a year older and built like a killer machine, we all call him Blood.

"What ya doin', Jones?" Blood's voice dropped back into its usual Blood growl.

One thing about Blood, he's impartial. He hates everyone. Except he hates me more than most. Don't know why. I puzzle and figure and still don't find the answer. Miz Lady says life is full of mysteries. I guess Blood's meanness is one of them.

"A garden!" Blood squeaked and clapped his hands. "How loooovely. What are we going to plant?"

I hoped those sudden switches from growling to squeaking would hurt his voice. You know, permanent laryngitis.

"Woses," said Ro, unplugging his mouth. "We're planting woses."

"Woses!" Blood howled. He slapped his leg. He laughed so hard, I thought he'd pee himself.

Gaby unplugged her mouth. She surveyed Blood.

"You're a giggling fool," she pronounced. Pop!—the thumb went back in.

"What?" Blood advanced.

Gaby unplugged her mouth. "You're a—"

"Never mind," I said.

"But he *asked*."

"What's the matter, Flower Boy? Afraid to let your little friend talk?"

"Jackson's not my friend," said Gaby. "He's Juana's."

"Juana's *boy*friend!" Blood clapped his

hand over his heart. "Jonesy, you never told me!"

"Really?" asked Gaby, gazing at me. "Do you kiss?"

"Shut up," hissed Juana.

Blood's palm shot out like a shovel blade and lightly smacked my cheek.

"You better keep your little friend in line."

"He's *not*—" Juana's hand clapped over Gaby's mouth.

Blood sauntered down the street, turned, and threw back: "Send me a rose, Bouquet Jones."

"His name's *Jackson*," Ro shouted.

I wheeled on Juana. "You said these kids have survival instincts."

"Giggling fool," muttered Gaby.

Juana grabbed Gaby's hand.

"Whyn't you hit him back?" Ro asked.

My face stung.

"Strategy," Reuben cut in. "Jackson's a *thinking* fighting man. He plans before he counterattacks."

"Huh," said Ro.

PLOT 5-1

"Here's the garden," I said, to change the subject.

I flipped the catch on the Rooter gate. The little kids ran through screaming, "Bouquet! Bouquet Jones!"

Reuben clapped me on the back. "Blood—what kind of name is that? Boy should be called Beetle-dung."

"Birdbrain."

"Burp."

We belched together. Loud.

Still, my face stung. "Bouquet Jones," shrieked Gaby and Ro. I hoped that stupid nickname didn't stick.

Reuben's eyes swept over the garden. I knew with his artist's eye he was seeing the green shoots against the smooth black earth.

Me, I was seeing all the work.

We found a stick with a small sign that read PLOT 5-1. My garden. A heap of tangled grass and weeds. Twenty-nine plots in Rooter's and mine was the weediest.

Then I looked down at my shoes. My Nike Air Jordans. Still almost new-shoe white.

I had wanted these shoes so badly. "Too

expensive," Mama had said. This is how I convinced her:

Me: "These shoes will save you money."

Mama: "How's that?"

Me: "They're school shoes, basketball shoes, church shoes—all in one pair."

Mama: "Whoa, Jackson. Are you going to wear sneakers to church?"

Me (patiently): "Not sneakers. Air Jordans. There's a big difference."

Mama (snorting): "Yeah, look at the price."

But she had bought them for me.

In that garden was dirt just waiting to mess with my shoes. I pulled off my Air Jordans and stepped into the plot.

Reuben unknotted the precisely tied bows in his laces. (Mama says every bow Reuben ties is a work of art. She asks him to tie things just to marvel at those bows.)

Reuben goose-stepped into the garden as if it were cold water. I pulled a handful of weeds and shook the clump.

"Hey, can we do that?"

Gaby and Ro tore off their beat-up sneakers and leapt into the garden feet first.

The little kids shook weeds at one another and giggled. The air smelled like onion grass and black dirt.

"Now we dig," I said.

Gaby lifted the spade. "What are we digging for? Treasure?"

"We're making a garden."

"Boring," said Gaby, walking away.

Ro paddled behind.

"*Don't* pick the flowers," Juana screamed after them.

Reuben and I decided to take turns digging.

I riffled through the first ten scoops.

Reuben dug the spade in deep, lifted the mound, turned it. Earthworms slithered off. One. The spade sank again, lifted, turned. Two.

My turn. The spade bit, flung, bit, flung, bit, flung. Finished.

Reuben's turn. He sank the spade, lifted it, turned the mound of earth.

Man, Reuben was slow. S-L-O-W. The weeds would be sprouting again before he finished. To take my mind off Reuben's slowness

I watched Gaby and Ro bugging Mailbags Mosely in his garden.

My turn. Lift, fling, lift, fling. My back ached from bending. The unturned dirt seemed to stretch out for about a mile.

"Jackson, all you're doing is throwing dirt around."

"At least I'm doing it faster than you."

"At least I'm doing it right."

"Yeah?"

"Yeah."

"You do it so good," I said, "do it all yourself."

Reuben paused. He grinned a big, big grin. He said, "It's your garden."

"Aren't we partners?" I said. "Sharing profits? Fifty-fifty?"

I was desperate. I pictured myself digging by the light of the moon. Alone. Lift, fling, lift, fling, lift . . .

"You boys need some help?" Mailbags Mosely loomed over us. Mailbags was the biggest man I knew. Gaby and Ro clung to him like goats to a mountain. His shovel would shame Paul Bunyan's.

Mailbags stepped into the garden. Dig, dig, dig, dig. The garden rolled out like a black carpet. He had even redug the part that Reuben and I had dug.

"Maybe he'll plant the seeds," I whispered to Reuben.

Mailbags showed us how to mix fertilizer into the soil and how to draw a thin, deep line in the dirt. Then he helped us sprinkle the seeds into the line and cover them. He dug a deep hole and stuck in the rosebush.

"Turn on the hose." He grinned at Gaby and Ro.

Fssst—the water shot out. Mailbags gave the seed lines a good wetting. Then he turned the hose on the little kids and washed their legs and feet while they jumped and chattered. Next he aimed the hose at our feet and had us hip-hopping. Last, he let the water rain down on his head. He looked like an elephant taking a bath.

"Again!" screamed Gaby and Ro.

"Gotta do my homework now," said Mailbags. "You want me to flunk college?"

"Yes!"

Mailbags winked at Reuben and me. "You should see results in a few weeks."

Great! I imagined blossoms waving gently in the breeze. One-dollar blooms and five-dollar roses.

Juana hauled the kids away from the water hose. They were spitting water like fountains.

"Juana," I said, "Reuben and I were wondering if you'd do us a favor."

"Like what?" She cuffed Ro.

"Could you talk to the seeds? You know, make them grow?"

"Do I look like a fool?"

"It really works," Reuben said. "Jackson's mother talks to her plants all the time."

"Let her talk to these plants."

"I don't want her to see the garden until her birthday," I said. "It's a surprise."

"I thought you were going to sell the flowers."

"That's *after* her birthday."

"Selling your mama's birthday present," said Juana, "is pretty cheap."

Stubbornness must run in the Rivera family, I decided. Juana could be as ornery as Gaby and Ro.

"Just say a few words," Reuben pleaded.

"Grow, plants," said Juana flatly.

"Try again," said Reuben, "with a little more enthusiasm."

"I can't scratch up a *shred* of enthusiasm," said Juana, "for a present that will be sold as soon as it's given." She stuck her nose in the air.

I rolled my eyes.

But Gaby and Ro had gotten into the planting spirit.

"Grow!" they screamed at the bare earth. "Grow, you dumb seeds!"

I figured such a welcome would either cause an instant blooming or scare those seeds deeper.

6

Reuben and I visited the garden every day after school. The results were:

Day 1: Nothing.

Day 2: Nothing.

Day 3: Nothing.

Day 4: Me: "Do you think something's wrong with these seeds?"

Day 5: Nothing.

Day 6: Reuben: "Maybe the seeds are dead."

Me: "How can they be dead? They haven't come alive yet."

Reuben: "Maybe Mailbags drowned them with all that water."

Me: "Maybe he'll have to plant our garden again."

Day 7: Nothing.

Day 8: All the other twenty-eight plots in the Rooter's Community Garden were sprouting.

Day 9: One tiny green shoot.

Reuben grabbed my arm like he had seen a Gila monster. "Look at that!" he yelled.

Then he waded into that dirt patch. He leaned way over like he was going to give that piece of green a big kiss.

"Reuben, it's just a plant."

"Ain't I got eyes?" he said, all huffy. "I can see it's a plant."

A one-dollar plant.

"Be careful, Bigfoot, you'll stomp our investment."

Reuben tiptoed out of the garden. "Maybe we should water it."

"You think so?"

Reuben considered the seedling. "Must be hard work pushing out of the ground. It could use a drink."

I stepped around the big puddle by the faucet, uncoiled the hose, aimed.

Water hit the seedling with the force of a hurricane.

Flattened it.

Reuben gazed into the mud. "You killed it, man."

"Maybe it'll pop up again."

"That plant is a goner."

I felt pretty bad. One dollar down the drain.

Reuben eyeballed me. "Ain't you going to fix it?"

"How am I supposed to fix a dead plant?"

But Reuben just crossed his arms and kept eyeballing me.

I pulled off my Air Jordans.

Squidge, squidge. The cold mud squeezed between my toes.

I looked all around. I didn't want anyone to see me cuddling a dead plant. I had my cool reputation to think of.

Juana was coming through the gate. Gaby and Ro hopped behind.

"Jackson Jones, Jackson Jones," they

shouted happily, "eats some bread to make his bones."

Juana shrugged. "They think they're poets."

"Juana, Juana, eats iguanas."

Juana ignored them. She turned to Reuben. "What's Jackson doing?"

"Fixing a plant he killed."

"I didn't kill it. I watered it."

Juana considered the plant. "Looks dead to me."

Gaby and Ro shrieked, "Plant murderer."

Very coolly I leaned over, dabbed some mud around the tiny shoot, straightened the leaves.

Whop! Something knocked me in the butt. The next thing I knew—mouthful of mud.

Gaby screamed with laughter.

Reuben leapt after her.

I jumped up, hit the garden path running. Yow! The wood chips dug into my bare feet. Gaby was a blurred dress weaving in the flower beds. Hop. Hop. Yow! Yow! I'd get her.

"Jackson's dancing," Ro screamed.

I dived. Reuben swiveled. We pinned Gaby like a muddy wildcat.

"Jackson loves Juana," Gaby howled.

"Leggo my sister." The voice was quiet, clipped. I looked up.

Legs apart, jaw set, Ro dangled one white shoe over the brown, oozing puddle by the faucet.

My Air Jordan.

"Juana," I yelled.

Juana leapt.

The next thing I saw: Juana clutching one white shoe.

The other sinking in the mud.

"You *hurt* me," Ro howled.

Then a familiar voice growled: "Bouquet Jones, looks like you done turned into a seed."

Very funny, I thought. I shook Gaby off. Refused to look over by the gate at that Blood Green.

"Boooo-kay loves Juana," Gaby screamed.

Head up, shoulders loose, I just kept walking. Very coolly. Yow! Yow! Those wood chips dug into my feet.

I picked my shoe out of the mud, wiped it on the grass.

"We were just leaving," said Juana.

"Me too," said Reuben.

I didn't answer.

As Juana herded the kids out, Gaby softly chanted: "Boo-kay's sneakers in the mud. Boo-kay's sneakers smell like crud."

Blood had already left. Gone to spread the news of my new name.

As I thumped my dirty shoe to the gate, Mailbags called, "I see you have your first weed."

"What do you mean, weed?"

"That weed." Mailbags thumbed at the one green shred in my garden. "You should pull it out. You don't want weeds crowding your flowers."

Great. I had killed a weed and then rescued it.

7

First one plant (weed), then two plants (weeds), then green leaves bombing all over the ground. Maybe weeds. Maybe . . . flowers.

"Dollar flowers," I said, surveying my business empire.

Only one corner of my empire was not cooperating. That rosebush. It looked like a pile of mean sticks.

"This thing should be busting with flowers." Reuben examined the thorns. "Maybe your mama should talk to it."

"Then my mama would be talking to her

birthday present. And I don't want her talking to her birthday present *before* her birthday."

Reuben kicked some wood chips. "I'm tired of this garden. Mud, plants, water. Water, plants, mud. When we gonna see some roses?"

Mailbags moseyed over. His garden looked as perfect as a picture in one of Miz Lady's magazines.

"Boys, you better pick out those weeds. Otherwise they'll choke your flowers."

"More work?" Reuben looked horrified.

"Which ones are the weeds?" I asked.

"Look for the biggest plants." Mailbags grinned.

My spirit dropped to the bottom of my Air Jordans, but I pulled off my shoes and waded into the garden.

"There's got to be an easier way," Reuben moaned.

"Just pull."

"Why don't we shoot a few hoops first?"

"Pull."

"Let's get a Mars bar. I got fifty-nine cents."

I kept leaning, pulling, tossing.

"I quit," said Reuben.

"You can't quit, you're a business partner."

"I quit anyway. Jackson, man, all you think about are these one-dollar greens. You are obsessed."

I kept pulling.

"This garden is nothing, man. Look at that rosebush. A puddle of thorns."

Lean, pull, toss.

"I got some good ideas for Captain Nemo."

Lean, pull, toss.

"I guess I'll do the next Captain Nemo adventure myself."

I straightened. I was plenty mad. "Captain Nemo is nothing without my writing."

"We'll see about that."

"Besides, it'll take you forever to do the next story."

"Will not."

"Forever and a Sunday," I said. By now I was boiling mad. "You are slow, Reuben. S-L-O-W. We could have done a *thousand* Captain Nemo comics by now, but you're so slow."

"What do you mean, slow?"

"Look at your shoelaces," I said. Reuben looked down. "Such finicky perfect bows. I've seen you tie one bow six—no, eight times until it's perfect. Why don't you just *tie* your laces?"

Reuben kept looking down at his perfect bows. Then he turned and, still looking down, walked to the gate.

"I'll buy out your share of the garden," I yelled.

Reuben opened the gate.

"I don't care if you take over Captain Nemo," I hollered.

Reuben, looking down at those finicky bows, disappeared around the corner.

"Fine," I screamed.

"Fine," I muttered to the next weed. Yank.

Puddle of thorns. I'd show him. Yank.

Thinks he can write Captain Nemo—Ha! Yank.

I showed those weeds no mercy. Yank. Yank. Yank. What kind of best friend quits a business, takes over your writing, and insults you all in one Saturday afternoon?

No kind of best friend. Reuben and I were quits as business partners, Nemo creators, *and* best friends.

Finally, I limped home. My back ached. An interesting blister had formed on my thumb.

"Oh, Jackson"—Mama beamed—"you are enjoying your garden so much."

Yeah, right.

Mama set out some dinner. "I can hardly wait to see what's growing there."

"Mostly weeds," I muttered.

But to myself, I added: That garden's growing nothing but trouble.

And that garden continued growing trouble. Trouble and weeds.

The next day I shoved $2.57 into an envelope and stuck it under Reuben's door. No name, no note, nothing. A hostile business takeover.

On Monday I found a note taped to my door: *What about interest?* So I calculated ten percent of $2.57 for six weeks. That came to thirty-eight cents. I stuck thirty-eight cents under Reuben's door.

On Tuesday I got a picture of a perfect Captain Nemo. Inside the cartoon bubble were these words: "Written and Illustrated by

Reuben Casey." *Written* was underlined twice.

I wanted to rip the picture, right through Nemo's finicky helmet and finicky space armor, down to his finicky boots.

Instead I yanked weeds.

Wait till I'm rich. Yank.

I'll be swimming in basketballs. Yank.

Written and illustrated by Reuben Casey— Ha! Yank. Yank. Yank.

Miz Lady yelled over the garden fence, "Money keeps showing up under my door, Mister Cool. Must be the tooth fairy."

School wasn't much better.

Me passing Reuben with my frozen-cool face.

Him passing me with his Popsicle face.

Blood Green calling me Flower Boy, Sissy.

Blood drawing chalk flowers on the sidewalk.

Blood shrieking, "Boo-kay!" like a crazy parrot.

Each weed became a perfect picture of Blood's mean smirk. Yank. Yank. Yank.

"Don't you want to play basketball?" Mama asked.

"Gotta work."

"Don't you want to visit Reuben?"

"Gotta weed."

"Want to go out for pizza?"

"Can't till it's dark."

Mama was wearing her worry look a lot these days. "You certainly enjoy that garden."

Yeah, right.

That garden was growing nothing but trouble and weeds.

Even Abraham and Juana wouldn't help. Abraham said he had allergies and that the garden would be the death of him. (His mother's words.) Juana said that I'd treated Reuben like dirt and she wouldn't work for a cheating friend. (Her words.)

Yank. Yank. Yank.

Mailbags even started paying me to weed his garden. So did old Mrs. Groomsby.

That garden was growing trouble, weeds, *and* dollar bills.

And finally flowers.

One day a few buds. The next day—

BOOM! Zinnias zinging. Nasturtiums knocking. Marigolds gleaming like gold.

I just sat down hard. This garden would be some kind of present for Mama's birthday.

Then one day my weeds stopped growing.

I couldn't understand it. Mailbags's weeds still grew. Mrs. Groomsby's weeds still grew. But my flowers flourished without the hint of a weed.

"Why?" I asked Mailbags.

Mailbags fingered a marigold.

"Sometimes I see things," he said, "when I start my rounds in the morning. Mind you, morning mist moves like a ghost, so I can't be sure. But I *thought* I saw something in your garden."

"What?"

Mailbags looked down. "Maybe a boy." He scratched his ear thoughtfully. "Maybe your friend."

I snorted. "He's no friend."

"No?"

"No."

"Sure is doing a friendly thing."

"Now that I'm going to be rich, he just wants back in the business."

"Is that so?"

"And he stole Captain Nemo from me."

Mailbags squinted up at the sun. "That morning mist sure tricks the eyes."

I watched Mailbags mosey back to his garden.

"He called the rosebush a puddle of thorns," I hollered.

Mailbags turned. "Puddle of thorns." He chuckled. "That's a good description."

"Wait till it sprouts those five-dollar roses."

"Jackson," said Mailbags, "that bush is going to be a puddle of thorns for a while. Roses take a long time to bloom—five-dollar or otherwise."

I kicked the ground. "Four dollars and ninety-five cents for a puddle of thorns. What kind of investment is that?"

"A lousy one," said Mailbags, whistling off to his cucumbers.

What a rip-off, I thought. Next year I planned *not* to have a garden. I'd make sure Mama was clear on that before my eleventh birthday. T-shirt, sports stuff, money—no garden. Someone else could have those stinking roses.

But if I didn't have roses, at least I had plenty of one-dollar zinnias, nasturtiums, and marigolds. Surely enough for one basketball.

Mama's birthday was in two weeks.

Then no more flowers, no more garden, no more trouble.

Just me quick dribblin', dunking, scoring. Shooting hoops all summer long.

9

"**F**orty-eight, forty-nine," I mouthed. The zinnias tossed in the breeze.

"What ya doing, Jackson?" Gaby materialized suddenly, lugging the thumb-sucking Ro.

"Nothing," I said, losing count.

"You were doing *something*," Gaby said. "I saw your lips move."

"Does Juana know you're here?"

"Sure," said Gaby. "She says we can't go to the store with her anymore 'cause Ro breaks stuff. She said you'd watch us."

"Didn't break nothin'," Ro mumbled around his thumb.

"The juice bottle was slippery," Gaby explained. She pulled Ro's thumb out of his mouth. "Or so he claims."

Ro popped his thumb back in.

"I don't have time to baby-sit," I said.

"Were you *praying*?" Gaby persisted. "Jackson was praying," she explained to Ro. Ro nodded solemnly.

"I was *counting*. At least until you interrupted."

"Count away." Gaby sniffed. "Who's stopping you?"

I started again. Silently one-two-three . . .

"Forty-nine, sixty-four, three, eleven," said Gaby.

"One trillion, ninety-two, three," sang Ro.

I stopped.

Gaby looked innocently at me. "What'd I do? I was just counting. I can count. It's a free country."

I started again. Twenty-seven, twenty-eight.

"You're counting the flowers," said Gaby.

Thirty-four, thirty-five.

"Juana says you're going to sell your mama's flowers. She says you cheated your best friend."

Forty-two, forty-three, forty-four.

"Me, I tell her it's a hard world. A man's got to make money."

Fifty—"What?" I said.

"Also a girl and her small brother," Gaby continued.

"So now you think we're partners?"

"Could be," said Gaby. "If I like the deal." She squatted. "Kids like Ro can *help* a business, especially if they're small and cute." She gazed significantly at Ro.

He stared back, working his thumb.

I said, "Looks like he has a plug in his face."

Gaby tugged Ro's fist. He held tight. They struggled.

"Anyway," said Gaby, giving up, "the thumb-sucking's part of his charm." She surveyed Ro, spat on the hem of her T-shirt, wiped his cheek. "Just try us. Cut a few of those red things." She waved at the zinnias. "Set up shop. Business will boom."

"How much?" I asked suspiciously.

"This time free," said Gaby. "Next time we talk money."

I cut ten zinnias. Mailbags said thinning was good for a garden. So I wasn't exactly selling Mama's birthday present before she saw it—I was *thinning*.

Gaby dragged Ro to the street corner. She stuck three dandelions in his hair, swiped again at his face.

"Look cute," she commanded.

"I gotta pee."

"Hold it."

To me she said, "Better work fast."

"What do I do?"

Gaby rolled her eyes. "I thought you were the big businessman. You gotta yell, 'Get your fresh flowers here.'"

"We need a sign."

Gaby glanced at the squirming Ro. "There's no time."

Suddenly she screamed, "Fresh flowers, right here!"

An old lady almost dropped her groceries. "Goodness, dear, you scared me."

"Want to buy some flowers?"

"I don't think so, dear. Maybe tomorrow."

"They'll be *dead* tomorrow," said Gaby.

The old lady just looked surprised and shuffled off.

"Fresh flowers!" Gaby screamed at the passing cars.

No one stopped.

"Cheap jerks."

Ro was really squirming now. "Gaby," I said, "maybe we should take Ro—"

"Quiet," she hissed. Her lips curved into a sweet smile.

Coming toward us was a woman with hair as big and shiny as Captain Nemo's helmet. Amazing! Her lips were the color of zinnias and her eyes blue-painted up to the brow. A sweaty man lumbered beside her.

"Oh, Frank," crooned the woman. "Just look at these adorable children." Her perfume advanced on us like the prow of a battleship. I stepped back.

"These flowers would look great with your dress," Gaby said hopefully.

"Red flowers with this orange?" The lady tittered.

Her blueberry eyes swept over the zinnias and settled on Ro. By this time the little guy was wriggling like an earthworm. I felt sorry for him.

"What a precious child!" cried the lady.

A look of pain crossed Ro's face. "Gaby," he whispered.

"He's my brother," said Gaby. "Very well behaved."

The lady patted the dandelions on Ro's head.

"The flowers are on sale today," Gaby prompted. "One dollar a flower. Ten dollars for the bunch."

"That's not a sale," I whispered.

Gaby kicked me.

"Such a little businesswoman," said the lady.

She smiled at Gaby.

Gaby smiled back.

They looked like they were trying to out-smile each other.

The lady showed some more teeth. "Frank," she said.

Frank mopped his forehead. He pulled a ten-spot out of his wallet and gave it to me. He didn't even look at it.

Gaby's smile relaxed.

The lady smiled brilliantly all around and sailed off in the midst of her perfume.

"Phew." Gaby held her nose. "You mean people *pay* for that smell?"

"There you are." Juana pounced on Gaby. "What are you doing?"

"Selling flowers," said Gaby. "Jackson, give me my share."

I fished in my pocket and came up with sixty-two cents.

"Seven dollars," said Gaby.

"What?" I yelped.

Gaby eyed me coolly. "My payment."

"Juana," wailed Ro.

"You used these children." Juana turned on me, her dark eyes flashing.

"Gaby said she'd help for free—"

"Cheat," said Juana. "Selling your mama's present."

"Pay up." Gaby stuck out her palm.

"Big money man," Juana spat.

She grabbed Gaby's hand. Her sandals slapped furiously on the sidewalk.

"Seven bucks, Bouquet Jones," Gaby

screamed, pulling at Juana. "You owe me seven bucks."

I wandered back to the garden.

Counted the flowers. Sixty-nine.

Counted again. Sixty-seven.

Counted again. Seventy.

Funny how a ten-spot can weigh kind of heavy.

10

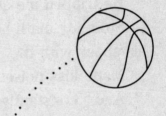

News travels fast when a man makes money.

Some people are happy. "Mr. Cool is successful!" Miz Lady bellowed in the hall.

Some people are skeptical. "Tell me again how you got that money," said Mama.

Some people are angry. "Cheat," Juana hissed whenever she saw me.

Some people are silent. Frozen-faced Reuben.

Some people are mean. Blood Green.

All those happy, skeptical, angry, even silent people I could deal with. Mean was a different matter.

After I sold my first bunch of flowers, Blood seemed to get even meaner. On a mean scale of 1 to 10 Blood usually hovered at about 9.5. Suddenly he was a 13.

He tripped me at recess.

Stole my math homework once and wiped his shoes with it.

Made kiss noises behind my back.

And constantly whispered, screeched, cawed, "Bouquet Jones! Bouquet Jones!"

These days at school everyone called me Bouquet Jones.

My cool reputation was shot.

The day Blood calmly flattened my sandwich, I had had about enough. First, tuna (with celery and lots of mayonnaise) is my favorite. Not to mention that his method of flattening was to sit his big butt square on my lunch. Then hand it back to me. Then smirk.

I spent all of English class fantasizing how I was a superhero who didn't know he was a superhero. But then some injustice—like having my lunch squashed—triggered a surge of power. In my best fantasy my arms grew meatier, my legs mightier, my brain brainier, and my eyes emitted powerful rays. And guess who I tackled first?

After school I moseyed to the garden, mostly to examine my crop and comfort myself. Mailbags was there, checking his cucumber vines.

As I've said before, Mailbags is huge. He could be his own mail truck. He always looked kind of funny stooped over his leaves, like a buffalo smiling at a violet.

He turned his buffalo smile to me. "You're looking wrung out, little man."

Now, I'm not one to blab my troubles, but my mind was so full of Blood and his Bouquet Jones that I blurted, "Why is Blood such a jerk?"

Mailbags fingered a bean blossom. "Some people get mean when someone has something they want."

I almost fell over. "Blood Green wants a garden?"

"Maybe he's just wanting."

"He's *wanting* to pick on me."

" 'Fraid so."

I stubbed the dirt.

"The way I see it," said Mailbags, adjusting his tomato cages, "you got three choices. Number one: fight him."

"That's suicide."

"Ignore him."

"I've been doing that. It doesn't work."

Mailbags pulled a stray weed. "Or you can dig up your garden."

"Dig up seventy dollars' worth of flowers?"

Mailbags shrugged. "There'd be nothing to make you different then," he said. "No one jealous. Everyone the same."

"Is Blood jealous?"

"He's wanting something that you have," said Mailbags. "He's looking for an excuse to be mean—some folks are like that. Your problem is, how you gonna handle it?"

Thanks for stating the obvious, I thought.

Mailbags unwound and carefully rewound the twine around the bean plants. "People mess with you even when you're grown," he said. He kept monkeying with the twine. "Some folks at the post office are always in my face saying, 'College, man, you are too *old*.

You learning little numbers. What good is that?' "

I couldn't imagine anyone being fool enough to mess with Mailbags. He could just scrape them off the way a buffalo brushes flies. Lay some big fists on them.

That's what I'd do to Blood. If I had big fists.

"So, what do you do?"

Mailbags considered a moment. "Still going to classes," he said, picking up the spade. "Still learning those little numbers they laugh at."

I watched as he loosened the dirt around his squash plants. Seems like Mailbags grows every weird vegetable in the world.

"You still see Reuben, you know, in my garden early in the morning?"

"I thought that was the mist."

"Do you see him?" I persisted.

"That time of morning I don't see so well," said Mailbags. "Why don't you ask him?"

I stubbed at the dirt.

"Jackson, please don't rearrange my garden with your big shoes."

I stopped stubbing.

Dig, dig, dig, went Mailbags's spade.

"I'm right, he's wrong," I said.

"Indeed."

"He started it, saying he wanted to quit."

"It's always that way."

"Reuben *is* slow. I was only speaking the truth."

Dig, dig, dig, went Mailbags's spade.

I stomped off.

Anyway, I got no time for thinking about Blood, that flashy-eyed Juana, and Reuben, my former friend.

I got to fix up the garden for Mama's birthday.

I smoothed the wood-chip path, watered the flowers, searched for weeds. No weeds.

Three more days—and Mama would have her present.

Four more days—and I'd have my present. Been waiting since April 10, my official birthday, for this basketball. Then a whole summer of dribbling, slam-dunking. One-on-one. Me against myself. All summer. I'd finally play someone who wasn't S-L-O-W.

Two days before Mama's birthday I was out the door early, racing the long way to school to check out the garden. Maybe catch a glimpse of that morning-mist boy seen by Mailbags. Maybe talk to him. Maybe not.

The wet grass clung to my one white and my one mud-stained shoe. The lemon sun had shined up the gate latch. Wood chips crunched in the quiet. Some birds chattered.

The garden.

I couldn't believe what I saw.

The garden.

I sat down hard. Drew my knees close.

Somewhere a woodpecker: tat-tat tat-tat-tat. Silence.

Who could be that mean?

I knew someone who could be that mean.

11

Leaves rustled, stems waved in the breeze.

No flowers.

My garden looked like someone had carefully sliced each flower from the top of its stem. Taken a pair of scissors, maybe, or a knife. Chop, chop, chop.

Seventy bucks gone.

Seventy flowers gone.

Those bare stems waving, waving.

My Basketball City summer just drained out of me. Ball, Mama's present—gone.

I sat for a long time. Till I was late for school. Then I sat some more.

I was tired of such meanness.

Tat-tat-tat. Silence. Tat-tat-tat. Silence.

I told my teacher, Ms. Wanbe, I was late because I woke up sick. She said did I want to go to the nurse. I said no. She said take out your reading book.

The whole time I read, I plotted my revenge. I felt superhero strong. Just wait till recess.

I glanced over at Reuben. He didn't look too good. I knew he knew about the garden, my mama's present, everything.

I wished I could tell him what I was going to do.

Reuben, I wanted to say, in case you never see me again, I *give* you my share of Captain Nemo.

I'd give Mailbags my spade.

Juana that ten-dollar bill.

Mama the puddle of thorns.

I was so busy planning my last will and testament, I missed Ms. Wanbe's first signal for recess. I scrambled out of my chair.

We marched down the hall.

My heart pounded. Lub-dub, lub-dub.

I'd never noticed before how a heart—my heart—makes a kind of music. I didn't want that music to stop.

What had happened to my superhero strength? All I had left was anger—and fear.

Anger and fear flopped back and forth in my stomach.

I shuffled across the blacktop, past girls jumping rope. Lub-dub.

Shuffle, shuffle, shuffle.

I was a lub-dubbing missile, right on target.

Steering toward Blood's big, mean head.

Blood's mean, laughing mouth.

Wham! I let him have it. Right in that mouth.

I saw the surprise in his eyes before he went down.

I jumped him. Wham, wham, wham. Ribs, nose, ribs.

Then I was on my back. His big face sneered over me.

Kids screamed.

Wham. This time my face. Sweet blood rushed in my mouth.

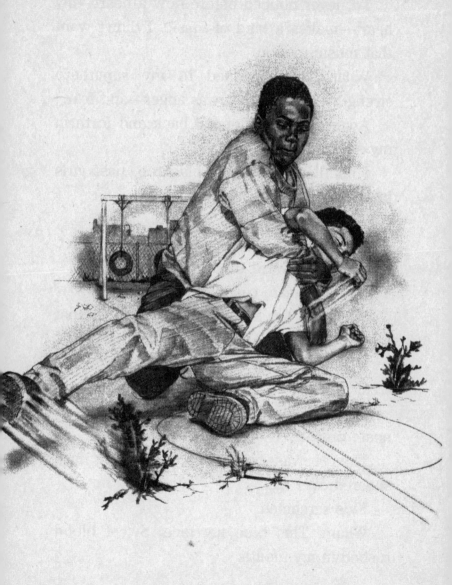

Somewhere Ms. Wanbe. "Boys! Boys!"

She hauled us apart.

"Who started this fight?"

Blood sneered. I spat. The other kids were silent.

Ms. Wanbe hauled us to the principal's office, where he steepled his fingers at us.

"Little punk jumped me," Blood told him. "I don't know why."

"What about my garden?" I said.

"I know nothing about your garden."

"Liar."

"Boy, you are dead already," said Blood. He calmly spiraled a tissue up his nose.

The principal sent us home early. Mama picked me up and I left Blood slouched in his hard-backed chair. He still had that tissue cocked from his nose.

Mama started the car.

Then she started in on me.

"Jackson, you better tell me why you are sitting in this car and not in that schoolroom."

"Got in a fight."

"And why did you get in a fight?"

"Guy made me mad."

"That's not like you, punching people. All this spring you've been happy in your garden—"

"That garden's nothing but trouble."

"Jackson!"

"I'm going to dig it up."

Mama's hands tightened on the steering wheel.

"Destroy it."

"Fine," said Mama. "Destroy it. Just keep out of fights. I can't be hauling you home every other day."

A squirrel shot into the road, leapt, dived up a tree.

"This city is no place for a boy. All this fighting, violence, drugs." Mama was talking to herself. "I try to give you a safe neighborhood, a little piece of country . . ."

"Mama," I said, "I didn't want a little piece of country. I wanted a basketball."

"Fine," said Mama, wobbling the wheel.

I stared out the car window. Streetlights, sidewalks, apartment buildings. In front of some town houses, little strips of flowers. Zinnias, marigolds, pansies. Last year they'd have been only colored blobs. Now I knew their names.

"Jackson," Mama said. Her voice sounded squeezed, like she was trying not to cry. "Didn't you like the garden even a little?"

Then out came the whole story: Reuben, business partner. Reuben, ex–business partner. Blood Green. Bouquet Jones. Puddle of thorns. No weeds. Seventy bucks. Birthday surprise. Lost flowers.

"Not lost," I said. "Killed."

Mama rolled down her window. "You were giving me a wonderful birthday present," she said. "I can just imagine the smell of those flowers." She breathed the city air deeply, coughed.

"The zinnias didn't really smell that great," I said.

"Never mind. I know they were beautiful."

We passed silver and glass buildings, brick fronts, card stores.

"When I was pregnant"—Mama broke the silence—"I couldn't decide whether to name my baby—that's you—after my favorite flower or my favorite horse."

"What's your favorite flower?"

"Rose."

"I'm glad your favorite horse was Jackson."

Mama laughed. We passed some trees, pigeons, more flowers. I even saw zinnias. The red ones sort of reminded me of Juana. She has this red church dress that's so stiff, it sticks out in layers. Like a zinnia. Funny how I'd never noticed that before.

Mama suddenly giggled. "Who would have thought my baby would turn out to be not just a single flower—but a whole bunch." She giggled again. "Bouquet Jones."

I rolled my eyes.

"Bouquet Jones." Mama sniffed and coughed at the June air. "Where's a good place for my birthday dinner?"

That's how Mama and I came to celebrate her birthday at the Space Shuttle Grill, where the soft ice cream comes in flying saucers.

Reuben would have loved it. I could hardly wait to tell him.

If I told him.

Yeah, I decided, I'd tell him. And right after

he apologized, I'd even give him my flying saucer.

Riding home, I was full of good thoughts.

I'd punished Blood.

I'd forgiven Reuben. Well, at least in my heart. Tomorrow I would forgive him in person.

I'd given my mother a wonderful birthday present. She said so.

"Mama, do you mind that I was going to sell your birthday flowers to buy a basketball?"

Mama shook her head.

"I was giving you the *look* of the flowers," I explained.

"You were very clear about that."

I felt a surge of generosity. "The basketball costs twenty-four ninety-five," I said, "so maybe I could just sell twenty-five flowers. That way you could see the flowers for longer than just your birthday."

I shifted in my seat. The city sped by.

"That is, I could have done that if the flowers hadn't been stolen."

All Mama said was "Flowers grow again."

I went to bed feeling good.

The next morning I woke up feeling sad.

I remembered the look of those bare stems.

Then, as if I had to torture myself, I dragged on my jeans, left a note for Mama, and slipped out the door.

I took the roundabout way to school again.

Slapped through the wet grass, opened the gate latch.

Bird chatter. Woodpecker tat. Crunch of wood chips.

Then I stopped.

The garden.

I couldn't believe it.

12

On each green stem—seventy to be exact—was a small, colored bow. Red bows. Yellow, blue, purple, white bows. Each bow tied precisely.

Finicky bows.

Perfect bows.

There were even bows—I counted twenty-six—on the rosebush. They nestled in that mess of barbed sticks like little birds waiting to sing.

Only one person could make bows like these.

I could picture him measuring and cutting the ribbon, tying the knot, looping the rabbit ears, pulling. Maybe even untying the bow, looping it into perfection. It must have taken him hours. He was that slow. That precise.

My man, Reuben.

For the second day in a row I was late to school.

"I suppose you were sick again," said Ms. Wanbe.

"Yes'm," I said.

"But you're feeling better now."

"Much better."

Ms. Wanbe sighed.

All during reading I waved at Reuben, made imaginary bows in the air.

"Jackson," said Ms. Wanbe, "you may be feeling too good."

"Oh, no, Ms. Wanbe, just good enough."

Ms. Wanbe sighed again and signaled for recess.

I caught up with Reuben, started walking real slow.

"Blood's going to kill you," said Reuben. "You better be glad he's not here today."

"Blood, Blood, Blood—is that all you can say? Where's my big hello?" I was joking but feeling nervous at the same time. Not about Blood—about Reuben. See, I'd been so bent on winning our fight, proving I was right, that I'd forgotten, well, that Reuben was my friend. Now he does this nice bow-thing—and I feel like all this time I've been trying to win a race that wasn't even a race.

I did not feel cool.

"Thanks for the bows."

"It's nothing, man. Woolworth's had a sale."

Still walking. Slow.

"Miz Lady wants to bring your mama's birthday cake to the garden. That okay?"

More walking.

"We could be partners again," I said. "Except the garden's not much now."

More walking.

"How you doing with Captain Nemo?"

"Okay," said Reuben. "Miz Lady said my last strip was great."

My spirit sank to the toes of my Air Jordans.

"She said the drawing was very detailed"—

Reuben eyeballed me—"but the writing had lost its spark."

My spirit leapt up past my knees.

Suddenly Reuben bonked my head. I poked his arm. And before I knew it, I had promised him my Space Shuttle Grill ice cream saucer.

"Reuben," I said, "I'm sorry I said you were slow."

"Precise," said Reuben.

That's how Mama got two birthday celebrations in a row—one at the Space Shuttle Grill and one at the garden.

She liked Reuben's bows. She liked Miz Lady's pineapple surprise cake. She liked Mailbags's gift of two crookneck squash.

She loved the flowers I bought from the florist. Even though they were a rip-off. Ten dollars for two wrinkled yellow roses and a tuft of leaves.

Abraham even came.

"I thought a garden would be the death of you," I said.

"Just came to sing happy birthday to your mother."

"I hope you can stay for cake," said Mama.

"I hope so too," said Abraham.

Abraham ate his usual two slices of cake. I didn't even tease him, I felt that good.

"I even got myself a present." Mama laughed and waved a package of zinnia seeds. "I'm hoping Jackson will share a corner of his garden."

"Garden's dead," I said.

"No way," said Mailbags. "Those flowers are going to bloom again. Give 'em a few weeks."

Seventy flowers blooming. Twenty-five spelling *basketball*.

Reuben and I high-fived.

"Here comes Juana and the kids," said Mama. "Maybe they'd like some cake."

Slap, slap, slap. Juana's sandals marched up the garden path. In one hand she carried a peanut jar and a plastic grocery bag. The other was clamped to a struggling Gaby.

Slap, slap, slap. Juana's face was set.

"She doesn't look like she wants cake," Reuben whispered.

I knew that look. Juana had turned that same look—THE LOOK—on me when she had accused me of cheating Gaby.

"The money's gone," I shouted. "I bought flowers for Mama's birthday."

Slap, slap, slap, slap.

Juana halted in front of me.

"Gaby has a confession to make."

So THE LOOK was directed at Gaby, not me. What a relief.

Gaby scrambled for the peanut jar. Ro dove for the bag.

Juana shook them off.

"A terrible confession," she said.

"They're mine," Gaby screamed. "Mine, mine, mine."

As I watched Gaby claw and leap, I had a terrible feeling. My spirit fell again and landed somewhere in the heel of my right Air Jordan. It trembled there.

I had punched the wrong man.

13

"What's in the jar?" I asked Juana.

"Olive oil."

"*Fragrant* oils," howled Gaby.

"She was making perfume," Juana explained.

I grabbed the bag. It was full of petals. And broken flower heads. Probably about seventy.

"You stole my perfume"—Gaby landed a kick on Juana's leg—"just when it was smelling good."

"Smelling good," Ro howled.

Gaby sighed tragically. "I was going to sell it for a hundred bucks a bottle. Maybe more. It smelled much better than that blond-head lady's." She faced me. "I was going to cut you in on the profits, Jackson. Honest. Just as soon as I invented it."

Juana's face didn't change expression.

Gaby gazed out across the garden as if seeing a great vision. "I was going to call it Bouquet Jones," she said. Her look swept across the street, as if including the cars, people, and 7-Eleven store in her vision. "It would have been as famous as Calvin Klein perfume. Now . . ." She sadly spread her empty hands.

Mama uncapped the peanut jar. Sniffed. "Vanilla," she pronounced.

"A hint of cinnamon," said Miz Lady.

Mailbags sniffed. "Definitely olive oil."

"And twelve drops of Night of Stars," said Gaby. "Dab some behind your ears. Free trial."

"Gaby has three dollars and seventy-two cents, which she would like to pay you for damages," Juana told me.

"No, she wouldn't," said Gaby.

"It's okay," I said. "The flowers will grow back."

Gaby stuck her tongue out at Juana.

"Just don't ever cut them again," I added quickly.

"The perfume business is bust anyway," said Gaby. "Mama locked up the Night of Stars."

"Aren't you forgetting something?" Juana directed THE LOOK at Gaby.

"Cake?" Gaby asked.

"Apologize to Jackson."

"No."

THE LOOK deepened.

"I'm-sorry-I-cut-your-stinking-flowers-now-can-I-have-some-cake." Gaby got that out in one breath.

"I'm sorry," said Ro.

"Ro didn't do anything," said Reuben.

"He just wants cake," explained Gaby.

Juana turned to Ro. "Say, 'please,' not 'I'm sorry.' And don't suck your thumb."

"I'm not sucking, I'm *tasting*."

Juana addressed the adults. "I'm trying to teach them manners."

Then Juana apologized to me, saying she had falsely accused me of cheating Gaby. Seems like Gaby finally told her the real story behind the sale of the red zinnias. She also said she still felt—THE LOOK crossed her face—I had treated Reuben wrong.

I knew that.

Night was coming on and the lightning bugs dipped over Reuben's bows. Checking out the exotic flowers, I guess. Still we stayed outside. Mailbags rapped in his buffalo voice about a dude that sowed seeds and reaped gold—mari-gold. We all laughed. The little kids sang about *el gato* in a sombrero. (Which means "cat in a hat." Juana's taught me that much Spanish.)

Then I started thinking how we—Reuben, Miz Lady, Juana, everybody—were gathered around kind of like the plants in my garden. Like flowers, almost. (Except Gaby was more like a weed.) And the city Mama and I had passed through last night—with folks sitting on their front steps and pigeons and all—was part of that garden, and that garden spread out a long way in the darkness, even into other countries. It was weird to think of the garden covering that much ground. Like thinking of the sky making a place for everyone to breathe. And the vastness of space.

I thought and thought, trying to understand.

Big things and small things—how they all fit together. How flowers die—and then come back. (According to Mailbags, anyway. I'd believe *that* when I saw it.)

Mama told a story. Miz Lady told a longer one.

Till the mosquitoes started biting and drove us inside.

Mama said it was her happiest birthday ever.

The next day as Reuben and I walked to school, he asked the BIG question:

"You scared about Blood?"

I'd asked myself that question a lot since Mama's garden party.

"I know what I'm going to do."

"Prepare to die." Reuben shuffled beside me. "Hey, can I have your Nemo notebook when he wastes you?"

"He's not going to waste me." Lub-dub. My heart again.

"How about your spade?"

"Vulture."

"Dead meat."

Reuben softly punched my arm.

At school Blood eyed the clock, then eyed me, then eyed the clock. He reminded me of a Doberman pinscher watching a little piece of steak.

Ms. Wanbe signaled for recess.

Grim-lipped, Reuben walked beside me. We were the last in line.

Lub-dub, lub-dub went my musical heart.

One by one the kids peeled off to the blacktop.

Except Blood. He waited for me by the door.

With the fat lip I'd given him, he looked twice as mean.

"Jackson," Reuben whispered.

"Shut up," Blood growled. "Or you're next."

He rubbed his fist into his palm. I wondered if he was going to lick his chops, like a Doberman pinscher.

"I got something to say." I stepped forward.

"You got *nothing* to say." Blood spat. The spit quivered, then seeped into the sidewalk.

"I know you didn't cut those flowers."

Blood stepped back. His big face seemed to deflate. "I never touched your stupid garden."

"I know," I said.

"So apologize."

"I'm sorry."

"Jackson, you fool," Reuben wailed.

Blood glared at me. "Is this a joke?"

I shook my head.

Blood peered into my face. "Are you scared?"

"Only a little," I said honestly.

Then Blood doubled back and—Wham!—punched me.

But on the arm. And not too hard.

"See you don't make that mistake again." He sauntered off.

Reuben grabbed me. He pawed me like I

was that guy in the Bible, Lazarus, come back from the dead. "You okay, man?" he kept asking.

I straightened my arm. It worked just fine.

I stepped into my walk, the one Miz Lady calls my Mr. Cool style.

"That boy's just wanting," I said.

I wish I could say Blood never bothered me again. But he still cawed "Boo-kay" over the garden fence, and once in a while he'd punch my arm, for old times' sake. His meanness continues to be one of life's mysteries. Maybe someday he'll find out what he wants.

The flowers grew back, just like Mailbags said they would. And with three people—Reuben, Mama, and me—working that garden, I had more time for other things.

Hanging out.

Writing three Captain Nemo strips.

Slam-dunking my new b-ball.

Yes, the day finally came when I trimmed twenty-five zinnias. Reuben tied up their stems with a precise bow. And Mailbags bought the whole bunch. Just slapped twenty-five bucks in my hand and lifted those zinnias high. "These flowers are perfect," he said, and smiled his buffalo smile.

Reuben and I stepped down to Harvey's Sports and tapped, poked, and softly dribbled each basketball. Then we tapped, poked, and dribbled them all over again. I'd waited for this basketball for a long time. I wanted to make sure I bought the best.

Finally, I laid down my flower money and picked up the best basketball. I spun it, tossed a fast one to Reuben.

Thonk, my man caught it. Tossed it back.

Thonk, the ball slapped my palm. Ahh! That felt good.

And don't you know, when I got home those same flowers were sitting in Mama's blue vase.

"Did you buy those zinnias from Mailbags?" I asked.

"They were a gift," said Mama.

"Mailbags *gave* you those flowers?" I couldn't believe it. "Those flowers cost him twenty-five dollars—and he just gives them away. The man *wastes* money."

"Maybe not," said Mama.

After that I noticed that Mailbags tended to mosey over to my garden every time Mama was around. I also noticed Mama would stop weeding and chat.

"What kind of role model inclines a mama to laziness?" I grinned at Mama one day as we weeded the lettuce.

"Boy"—she grinned back—"you trying to grow trouble in this garden?"

But I knew better. Mixed in with trouble was some good garden stuff. I coolly yanked a weed.

About the Author

Mary Quattlebaum directs a creative/reminiscence writing program for senior adults in Washington, D.C., and teaches creative writing at Georgetown University, local schools, and libraries. She received the Novel in Progress/ Judy Blume Grant from the Society of Children's Book Writers and Illustrators and has been published in *Children's Digest*, *Spider*, *Cricket*, and *Ladybug*. *Jackson Jones and the Puddle of Thorns* is the winner of the first annual Marguerite de Angeli Prize.

About the Illustrator

Melodye Rosales studied art, filmmaking, and animation at the University of Illinois, the School of the Art Institute of Chicago, and Columbia College. She has illustrated several books for children, including *Kwanzaa*, *Double Dutch and the Voodoo Shoes*, *Beans on the Roof*, and *Addy* of the American Girl series. She lives in Champaign, Illinois, with her husband and two children.